# THIS BOOK BELONGS TO:

_____

Bluemont Tail: Roxy the Hanoverian Horse
An imprint of Mont d'Or Press
Text copyright © 2024 by Melina Macall
Illustrations copyright © 2024 by Kelly Weiner
Bluemont Equine Sanctuary name and logo used with permission from Bluemont Equine Sanctuary.
All rights reserved. Published in Montclair, NJ, USA. Printed in the United States of America.
No part of this book may be used or reproduced in any manner whatsoever without
written permission, except in the case of brief quotations embodied in critical articles and reviews.
Library of Congress Control Number: 2024903882
ISBN 979-8-9893969-0-0
For more information, media inquiries, live event bookings, or to request permissions, contact publisher:
Email: books@montdorpress.com          Website: www.montdorpress.com
FIRST EDITION

Young listeners and early readers can enjoy reading along with the audiobook.
Roxy the Hanoverian horse will neigh when it's time to turn the page.

Available at your favorite audiobook retailer and public libraries everywhere.

*Happy Reading!*
*Malina Macall*

In memory of my parents who introduced me to the world of books and the worlds within books.
To Hope, Noah, Gabe, and Tal whose joy of reading began with picture books.
To Martin, the best partner one could ever wish for.
- M.M.


To all my friends and family who supported me while working on this book.
To my parents Marc and Debbi who have encouraged my artistic pursuits since I was little.
In memory of Lisa Hunt who inspired me to create, pursue passions, and learn from mistakes.
- K.W.

*Enjoy the animals!*
*Kelly Weiner*

# BLUEMONT TAILS
## ROXY THE HANOVERIAN HORSE

WRITTEN by Melina Macall

ILLUSTRATED by Kelly Weiner

MONT D'OR
PRESS

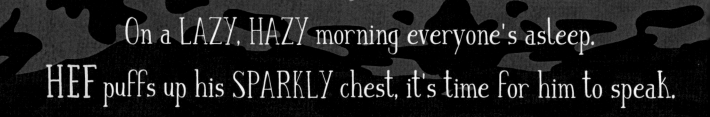

On a LAZY, HAZY morning everyone's asleep.
HEF puffs up his SPARKLY chest, it's time for him to speak.

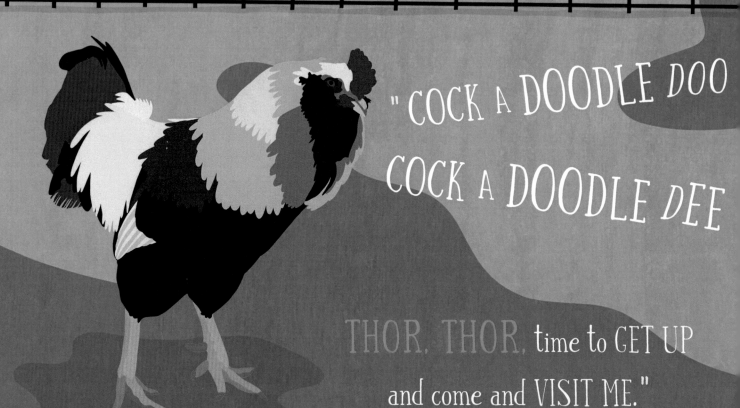

" COCK A DOODLE DOO

COCK A DOODLE DEE

THOR, THOR, time to GET UP
and come and VISIT ME."

SHAKE,
SHAKE,
SHAKE.

SHAKE,
SHAKE,
SHAKE.

A downward dog,
now THOR'S awake.
Yawn and stretch,
Stretch and yawn.
It's THOR PATROL TIME just after dawn.

"THOR PATROL, PATROL, THOR PATROL,

ONE, TWO, THREE!

Does EVERYTHING look GOOD to me?"

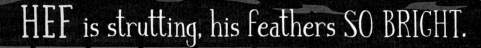

HEF is strutting, his feathers SO BRIGHT.

He PUFFS UP his chest with ALL HIS MIGHT.

"How'm I lookin'?

How'm I lookin'?"

"You look SO FINE!"

"I'm the FINEST looking rooster in ALL OF TIME."

"THOR PATROL, THOR PATROL,

ONE, TWO, THREE!
Is EVERYTHING fine, as FINE as can be?"

"Good morning, THOR,"
purrs MAMA CAT. "All good here."

"I'm glad of that."

"I have my kittens SAFE AND SOUND.
OH DEAR, now they're CLAMBERING around."

MEOW, MEOW, MEOW, rough and tumble,
MEOW, MEOW, MEOW, leap and fumble.

MEOW, MEOW, MEOW,
up and down,
MEOW, MEOW, MEOW,
round and round.

MEOW, MEOW, MEOW,
swing high, swing low,
MEOW MEOW MEOW,
WHEEEEE! Here we go!

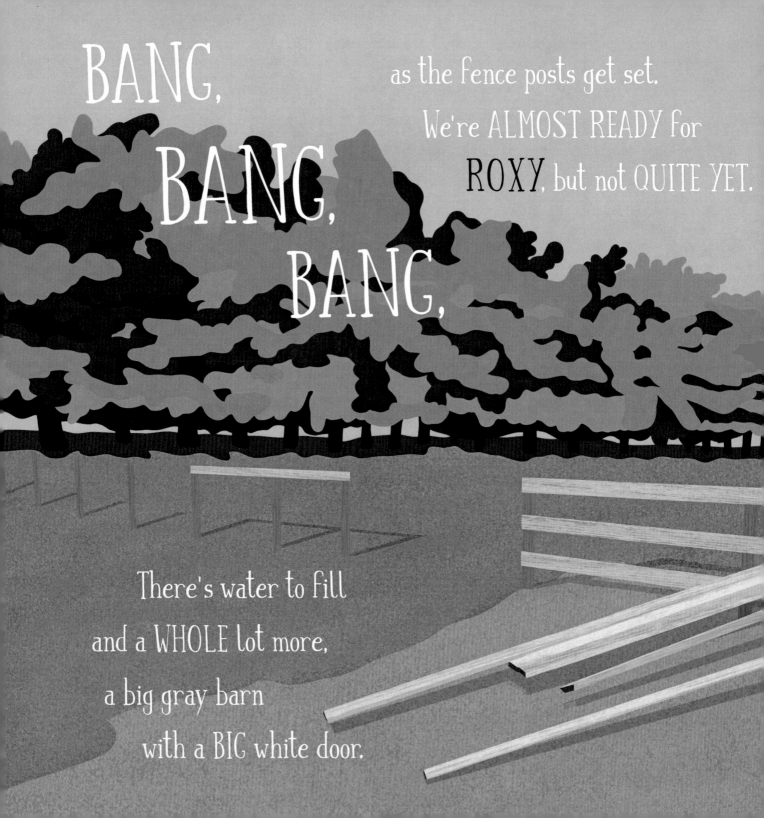

BANG,
BANG,
BANG,
as the fence posts get set.
We're ALMOST READY for
ROXY, but not QUITE YET.

There's water to fill
and a WHOLE lot more,
a big gray barn
with a BIG white door.

CLUCK, CLUCK, CLUCK!

CLUCK, CLUCK, CLUCK!

"HENNY PENNY, HENNY PENNY.

What's the din?"

THOR can't you hear, the sky's falling in."

"Not at all, HENNY PENNY, don't you worry. It's CARL with the trailer, I must HURRY!"

BEEP, BEEP, BEEP!

The gates swing aside.
Over the CRUNCHY gravel,
CARL drives inside.
He parks the trailer
and opens the back,
out steps ROXY,
so LARGE and so BLACK.

"Welcome to BLUEMONT your FOREVER home.

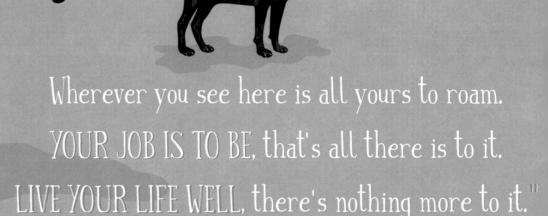

Wherever you see here is all yours to roam.

YOUR JOB IS TO BE, that's all there is to it.

LIVE YOUR LIFE WELL, there's nothing more to it."

ROXY was quiet, taking this in.
She was TIRED and HURTING,
and also quite THIN.

CJ came out and
gently stood there.
A NEW feeling descended,
there was PEACE in the air.

I'm so TIRED. I'm so LOW.
My tail is MATTED.
My eyes have no GLOW.

My back is ACHING. My skin is ROUGH.

My feet are sore. MY LIFE GOT TOUGH!"

"When was the last time you saw a DENTIST or VET?
We'll sort you out, ROXY, don't you fret.
We'll put FOOD IN YOUR TUMMY,
make your teeth NICE and BRIGHT.

My GOODNESS those hooves,
a pedicure's in sight!"

"There's lovely grass pasture,
feels good for my feet.
It's also delicious,
I can't wait to eat."

"We'll FATTEN YOU UP
with mash and fresh hay,
you'll soon FEEL MUCH
BETTER in every way."

APPLE
SAUCE

**MOM'S RESCUE FARM**
EST. 2019

MEDICINE

Antibotics

Vitamins

Wound Cream

Hoof Powder

Ointment

SLURP,

SLURP,

SLURP, the medicine is YUCKY.

Her leg is much better, ROXY feels LUCKY.

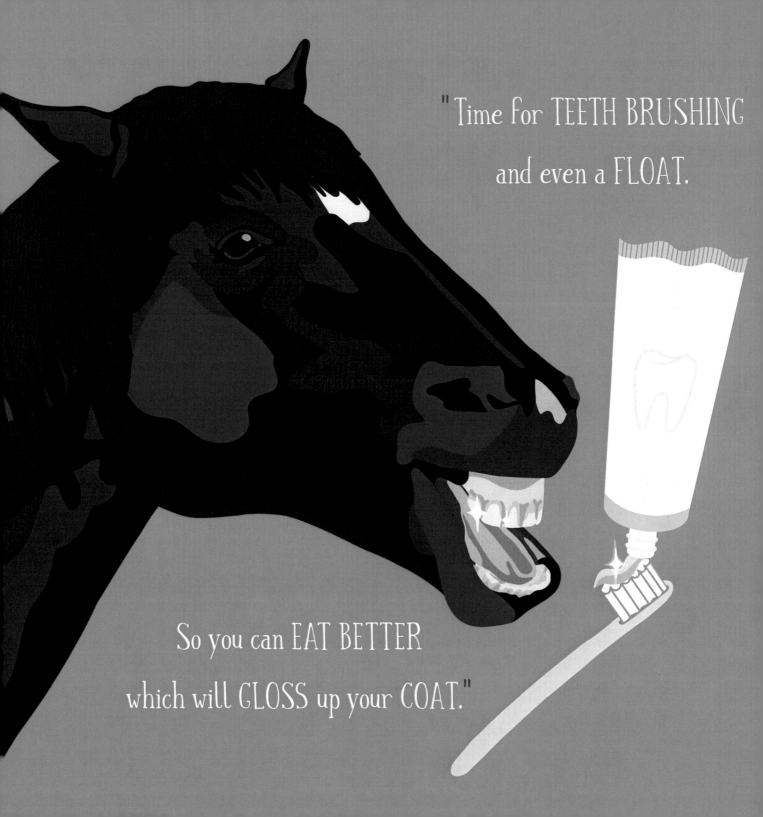

Something is MISSING, ROXY feels quite ALONE, she needs some more horses in her NEW HOME.

So LESLEY set out
to find ROXY some friends.
There were SO MANY OPTIONS,
the list never ends.

Those who were ridden,
and those who pulled carts,
those who did dressage,
race winners, and stars.

THOR was her HELPER
as she went through the lists.
He worked the computer,
he's quite GOOD at this.

BEEP, BEEP, BEEP! The gates swing aside,
over the CRUNCHY gravel
CARL drives inside.

Here's EVA and JUNA
for ROXY to meet.

ROXY'S heart soars,
NOW HER HOME IS COMPLETE.

ROXY'S so happy,
she runs with her friends,

there's TESS,
and FELORA,

and SPARKY,
and WREN.

With all these new horses, there's SO MUCH to do.
the SOUNDS on the farm make a HULLABALOO!

WOOSH,

WOOSH,

WOOSH,

putting out the hay.

WOOSH,

WOOSH,

WOOSH,

on such a LOVELY day.

FILL the water,
SPLISH, and
SPLASH,
then go MAKE
the horses' mash.

# SCOOP,

Scooping up the poop.

Scooping up poop is an ENDLESS loop.

WINTER,

SPRING

SUMMER

and
FALL,

ROXY stays outside, she just LOVES it all.

In her WARM winter blanket ROXY runs through the SNOW,
the mist of her breath, her eyes all AGLOW.

Horses and minis, donkeys and goats,
ALL HAVE A HOME HERE,
the young and the old.
Every one is special, every one has needs,

WE'LL LOVE YOU FOREVER,
that's the BLUEMONT creed.

COME BACK to BLUEMONT
and MEET MORE OF OUR FRIENDS.

The laugher, adventure, and FUN never ends!

# BLUEMONT SANCTUARY IS HOME TO...

## DONKEYS + MULES

Charlotte       Moses
Dixon           Rue
Gemma           Sully
Jax             Taz
Mason

## HORSES

Allister        Roseanne
Autumn          Roxy
Awesome         Sam
Beau            Shannon
Con "Tess"a     Sparky
Everest         Stevie
Fetora          Sully
Glowy           Sylvie
Jane            Viva
Jovie           Willie
M+M             Winnie
Nelson          Wren
Poet            Xena
Riley

## MINIATURE HORSES + PONIES

Bucky           Gracie
Buster          Hazel
Charlie         Juna
Cinder          Mama
Coco            Maverick
Daisy           Midge
Esme            Peanut
Eva             Silver Song
Firefly         Snowy
Gideon          Walter
Goose

## GOATS

Cupid           Odie
Flower          Prim
Hedwig          Puffin
Mochi           Pumba

## CHICKENS

Hef the rooster
Henny Penny
The Golden Girls

## CATS

Daisy
East
Mama Cat
Mimi
Speck
West
White Paws

## DOGS

Thor
Zoli

 FOREVER IN OUR HEARTS

## ROXY THE HANOVERIAN HORSE

Hanoverian horses are intelligent, calm, and eager to learn. Their temperament makes them an extremely popular breed. They are noted for courage and boldness and have a strong back, powerful body, athletic movement, and strong limbs.

Roxy is a beautiful 17.3 hand imported Hanoverian who had a successful jumping career for many years. Unfortunately, she wasn't offered a soft place to land for her retirement by any of her previous owners. She was no longer "useful" in the horse community because chronic lameness and arthritis prevented her from being able to do a job.

After many happy years at Bluemont living out her retirement with her friends, Roxy, sadly, passed away in 2023.

Roxy serves as the inspiration that Bluemont has blossomed into.

## BLUEMONT EQUINE SANCTUARY

Bluemont Sanctuary is a family run 501(c)3 Non-Profit Organization located in beautiful Colts Neck, New Jersey. Bluemont's story began in 2019 with the arrival of Roxy and has quickly grown into an organization that now provides a permanent residence to over 40 horses, donkeys, ponies, and goats who have been saved from slaughter, neglect, and abuse.

Bluemont's model is one of permanence. Every rescue that walks through the barn doors, stays for life. Each animal is provided with a soft landing, including acres to roam, plenty of hay to eat, any medications needed, and a herd and family to call their own.

Under this model, every animal gets to live as naturally as possible and will never be adopted out, ridden, or used in any way. Never again will they be subjected to the hardship that they once knew.

Learn more on Instagram @bluemontequinesanctuary

Lesley Luckhardt and Carl Quaglia,
co-founders of Bluemont Equine Sanctuary.

MELINA MACALL'S love of reading started when she was very young. Most nights she slept with a book under her pillow. *Noddy* taught her that everyday life offers adventures all the time. *Gerald Durrell* introduced her to the amazing world of animals, and a passion to respect and protect them. Instead of becoming a vet, her careers have spanned theater, writing, education, advocacy and travel. Melina loves playing with words. Inspired by her volunteering experiences at Bluemont Sanctuary she is thrilled to share this incredible place in her debut children's picture book.

Melina lives in New Jersey where her family has raised many Seeing Eye dogs including Imari (aka Murray) who is now a permanent family member.

Visit her at www.melinamacall.com

KELLY WEINER is an artist whose work uses abstract shapes and color to create playful imagery with the intention of bringing a smile to the viewer. Her background in painting, illustration, and design is driven by her passion for creating.

She is a lifelong animal lover and an art and travel enthusiast. Her advice for young artists is to keep creating, mistakes can only lead to new beginnings. Bluemont Tails: Roxy The Hanoverian Horse is Kelly's debut children's picture book.

Kelly lives in New Jersey with her sweet cats, Toulouse and Ophelia.

Visit her at www.studiopamplemousse.com

Made in United States
North Haven, CT
26 March 2024

50539881R00024